Oopsie Daisy

CHERI GIENGER

AuthorHouse™
1663 Liberty Drive
Bloomington, IN 47403
www.authorhouse.com
Phone: 1 (800) 839-8640

Published by AuthorHouse 03/27/2019

ISBN: 978-1-7283-0500-4 (sc)
978-1-7283-0501-1 (hc)
978-1-7283-0499-1 (e)

Library of Congress Control Number: 2019903281

Print information available on the last page.

Any people depicted in stock imagery provided by Getty Images are models, and such images are being used for illustrative purposes only. Certain stock imagery © Getty Images.

This book is printed on acid-free paper.

Because of the dynamic nature of the Internet, any web addresses or links contained in this book may have changed since publication and may no longer be valid. The views expressed in this work are solely those of the author and do not necessarily reflect the views of the publisher, and the publisher hereby disclaims any responsibility for them.

authorHOUSE®

For Buddy, with love

One day, my Grauntie was babysitting me. I dropped my Lego dinosaur on the floor and it came undone. I was very sad because Daddy had built it for me.

But then Grauntie said, "Oopsie daisy!"

I thought that was the funniest thing ever. Suddenly it was okay that my dinosaur had come apart.

The next day, Mommy was making cookies and dropped all the eggs on the kitchen floor. She was kind of mad.

I said, "Oopsie daisy!"

She started laughing, and then it didn't matter that there were eggs all over the floor!

Daddy was very late coming home from work that night. When he came running through the front door, he slipped and fell and everything went flying.

Mommy and I said, "Oopsie daisy!"

We *all* started laughing.

The next day, my friend Tommy came over to play with my toy trains. I accidentally knocked the track over, and Tommy got very angry.

I said, "Oopsie daisy!"

But Tommy didn't laugh. Instead, he told my mommy that he was going home, and out the door he went.

Tommy came over again the next day. We were practicing writing our names because we were going to kindergarten soon. Tommy couldn't stay in the lines and got very angry.

I said, "Oopsie daisy!"

But Tommy didn't laugh.

Tommy wrote his name again but, just as before, he went outside the lines. This time he looked at me and said, "Oopsie daisy!"

And we both laughed and laughed.

The next day at school, my teacher, Miss Amy, was writing on the chalkboard, and the chalk broke in half.

I couldn't help myself. I said, "Oopsie daisy!"

Miss Amy turned around and started giggling. She said, "I think you're onto something here, Buddy!"

Oopsie daisy sure makes everything seem okay.

When times get tough

And you feel sad,

Don't get mad and run away.

Simply say

"Oopsie daisy!"

To make your troubles go away!

Printed in the United States
By Bookmasters